Tick Tock

Tick Tock

by

MINASU

THE CHOIR PRESS

First published in the United Kingdom in 2018 by
The Choir Press

ISBN 978-1-911589-51-8

Contents

_____

I

In the sky, you and I

_____

Sitting at her desk she rested. A thriving plant of pristine purple leaves spilled out over the edge of a patterned porcelain pot. Sweet music filled the room. A lamp presided over the desk and its rays lent a warm glow to the golden veneer of a ticking clock. For as long as this lady had known, this clock had ticked and tocked and she had not heard it for many a year. Little did this lady know that there was life inside her small desktop clock. Perhaps if she had taken the time to assess the clock from each of its sides she would have noticed that this clock was constructed from glass panes, which slotted into the golden veneer in a very old-fashioned way indeed. In fact, this clock had been her mother's. The lady had inherited several items from her when she passed away. In all the time that had passed she had lived with the clock at the head of her desk and so she sat face-to-face with the heirloom each and every evening before bedtime. The front panel was a piece of glass constructed just as the other sides, save the bottom, which was made of tin. However, unlike the other glass panels, which allowed the curious to examine the fine mechanisms within, this one was opaque. Obscuring her view of nuts and springs and rivets and washers and all manner of splendidly delicate mechanisms was a white surface of an unidentified material. This white surface was adorned by roman numerals painted by hand. She would remember her mother as she looked at these numerals and marvelled at their beauty. Her mind wandered to the wonderful poise one must have to control a paintbrush so. And then, just when her mind had wandered to a world in which everyone exercised such control and how wonderful such a world would be, she stood up and said to herself, 'Time to hit the sack,' and off she went to bed.

'A good friend of mine is on his way over,' called a mushroom headed creature named Layak from deep within the clock's structure.

'Good!' came the response from Nico, another member of this strange species.

These creatures were so small it would only be correct to describe them as minuscule. But make no mistake! What they lacked in stature they more than made up for in number, for this species dominated the innards of the clock like none had done for aeons, sprouting from every last nook and cranny. On this occasion these particular mushroom headed creatures were having a party, a small one, but a party nonetheless.

'Who is it?' asked Nico.

'He's called Ben,' replied Layak, his shaggy, scaly cap concealing a filthy trail of liquid filled with spores slipping down his stipe beneath his shirt collar and soaking his suit thoroughly. 'Though I'm not sure if you're going to like him,' he said.

'Is he a good shroom?' asked Nico.

'Yes, really good,' the slippery fellow replied.

'Then I see no reason why I wouldn't like him!'

Nico smiled and turned towards Kristina, the host of the party and a false champignon if ever there was one. A small white toadstool, she sat on the sofa with perfect form smiling and laughing at just the right moment to relay that she understood all and everything her guests could say to her. She had a few lines prepared for conversations spanning the great works of literature to the minutia of her guests' current predicaments. In any case, another week at work had gone by and she was grateful to have good company at short notice. Nodding attentively she listened to Adriana, her longest-standing friend and a mushroom known for her beauty as her stipe seemed to go on and on and on again, and her cap! Oh, wonders never cease! Her cap swirled around her

2

stipe as a magnificent blood-red lampshade pirouettes about its base. Kristina used to envy Adriana but years of observing her travails had led her to reassess.

'He hasn't picked up my calls for days and I don't know what to do,' moaned Adriana as she sobbed meekly into her caramel blouse.

Kristina did not know what to do either. Everybody she called was always more than happy to answer. 'Stop calling him,' she suggested.

Nico's younger brother Lucas, the chestnut to his portobello, pushed open the front door to this tiniest of tiny apartments, though good-sized in the context of the kingdom it ought to be said, to the sound of a creak, which alerted Kristina et al to his arrival. He was with Archie, a popular figure in the crowd and a shroom with a cap that ebbed and flowed like chocolate-brown-coloured molasses but unlike molasses there was nothing slow about Archie. No, Archie was known to his contemporaries as a shroom bestowed with the greatest of intellects and the rarest of humilities. Everyone congregated between the landing and the hallway and reacquainted themselves with each other until Layak launched into his latest rant. This one had something to do with his professional successes and social shortcomings but no one was listening and Layak did not mind this one bit. Well, at least Archie had caught the tail end of this sorry tale and that was all it took for him to conjure up a thoughtful response. 'Perhaps you should try slowing down ... I love your intensity but it may be too much for some.' A flashing light, the kind you see front and centre on a police car's roof, blinded everyone in the apartment out of the blue.

'I can't stop oozing!' cried Layak and off he dashed to the bathroom.

The sound of a siren hushed Archie before he could ask Layak what he meant.

The doorbell rang and Nico sauntered over to answer it. He asked, 'Is that Ben?' on the intercom and was greeted with a groan followed by something that sounded like 'Who the fuck else is it going to be?' Ben leapt up the stairs and bobbed among the guests. A white t-shirt hung off his slender, well-proportioned stipe and a short, scraggly beard did its best to conceal a tired cap, almost as pale as the t-shirt.

Layak burst out of the bathroom and seemed to speak so quickly as to compress time itself – 'How are you mate it's really good to see you it's been so long!'

Ben had the look of a shroom disgusted to its very core. 'Fuck off you d-dirty imbecile,' he squawked with a hint of a stutter. Layak bit down on his jaw and when he was able to release it again he introduced Ben to Kristina and Nico. 'Fuck the pleasantries I can't be f-fucked,' shot Ben, whose agitated gait was making the party decidedly uncomfortable, though he was not perturbed in the least. 'Where are the bugles?' he shouted at the top of his lungs, shaking the very superstructure of Kingdom Clock. The glass panes of the kingdom's outermost walls rattled riotously and the rains roared down against those panes and pitty pattered as though that were all they had ever done. But this infernal racket did in fact cease after not so much time at all.

'Sorry about that,' Ben whispered. 'I'm Ben by the way,' he said, turning to Kristina. 'Nice to make your acquaintance.' Kristina smiled at his softness and exclaimed that she was pleased to make his also. Lucas skipped over to offer Ben a tiny bugle from a box that housed twenty at one time. Now the tally stood at seven. Ben thanked Lucas graciously and rewarded him by playing this tiny bugle so sweetly that the room was moved to a standstill.

'So, Ben,' Kristina went on, 'what is it that you do?'

Ben's bemusement was evident and he made his disdain for the host of the party as clear as broad daylight. 'Isn't it obvious?' he asked wearily. The room stood still. 'I play the bugle of course!'

Everyone let out a light sigh in unison at this most obvious of obvious facts that had somehow evaded them.

'He makes a shit tonne of money doing it too,' crowed Layak from the bathroom doorway.

'Fuck off you smelly mess of a shroom,' retorted Ben. 'He's not wrong, though. I am the most supreme and excellent of all bugle players to have ever ticked along in this giant clock of ours.'

This mightily bold claim astonished Kristina but she was entranced and shrieked, 'It is your passion to play the bugle – how wonderful it is to meet a shroom with such skill and good looks too! Oh, it is like a dream!' Archie nodded along and pondered the very essence of passion, while Lucas sat still perched on the corner of the sofa.

Ben was bemused once more. 'Passion? My passion is money! The bugle is but a means to an end.' Kristina baulked at the delivery but nodded at the sentiment. She believed it noble to pursue a passion but not shameful to confess to a lack of one. That required an altogether different type of courage, she mused. Taking a wine glass to her lips she paused before drinking and let the scent fall over her. She peered across the room at Nico, whose demeanour was unchanged since Ben's arrival. She remembered the orange she had been gifted on her eighth birthday and how Nico loved that story. He always asked her how old she was when she received the orange, even though he knew she would answer 'around eight.' Kristina had never seen an orange before that day. To hold it was an experience in and of itself – its skin was so shiny and taut! For a time she took the fruit with her wherever she went, until it lost some of its lustre.

'Did you eat it in the end?' Nico would ask. Kristina did not remember.

She sipped her wine. 'It was just an orange,' she thought.

The room was silent save for some silky jazz music spilling from the stereo. Ben was bored. 'Shut up everyone!' he yelled at the top of his lungs.

Adriana locked eyes with Ben, unsure what to make of him. Experience had taught her that shrooms who did not know what they wanted from life were less sure of themselves, yet Ben seemed to buck that trend. 'Oh come on Ben,' she said playfully, probing at the puzzle before her. 'You must want something else. Money can't possibly satisfy you!'

Ben yielded to her to the surprise of Archie but not of Lucas. 'You're right,' Ben conceded. 'If all I had were money I wouldn't be able to ask you out on a date but luckily I'm really good-looking too. Kristina even said so herself just a moment ago!'

Adriana's curiosity disintegrated into a sigh that went unnoticed to all but Archie. He rolled his eyes. It was not Ben's manner that bothered him. 'Politeness is a strategy,' he pondered. 'There's no reason why rudeness shouldn't be too.' Instead, he was fixated on the malaise hovering over his new acquaintance. Archie had been humbled time and time again in his quest for understanding the world and those creatures that inhabited it but such setbacks only stoked his curiosity. He was sure of one thing, though: Ben's boldness was something he never had and never would have. 'So do you do anything other than play the bugle?' he asked.

'I do everything! Whatever I do, I'm the best at it. I've always been the best. Since day one – the best.'

Archie was unconvinced by Ben's vagueness so he pressed on with his examination – 'Care to give an example?'

Kristina was upset with Archie and she made it known by telling him to show more respect to the guests.

'I'm a guest too!' reasoned Archie.

But Kristina was having none of it. 'You're not a guest like Ben is a guest.'

Deeply sorry, the shroom of the undulating molasses muttered under his breath, 'Well he is new I suppose.'

The railway tracks echoed under the rocking of carriages hurtling through the night and car tyres skidded through puddles the length and breadth of all of the streets in the neighbourhood. Nico had been left cold by the aforementioned exchange between Kristina and Archie. He solemnly stared out of the window and gazed for miles and miles to the very edge of Kingdom Clock but all he could see was darkness. 'Archie is invaluable at events such as these,' he pondered over the epic puddle before him. 'She just doesn't understand,' he thought. It was Archie's role to make sure guests were at ease and stimulated by an array of poignant questions which would reach from physics to philosophy and back again. 'But you have to start with the small things – and that's what Archie was doing!' In any case, he kept these thoughts to himself and returned to his role, which was to ensure the guests had everything that they could possibly need at any given moment. 'Hey Ben!' he called. 'Do you play pint-sized bugles as well?'

And at that Ben's eyes lit up with all of the clarity of the midday sun. 'Of course!' he screamed with the utmost joy.

'Wonderful,' said Nico, already making for the kitchen to retrieve a fitting bugle for a man purported to be a master of this realm and also, lest we forget, the newest addition to the group.

***

A saxophone solo hummed through the living room and the lady rolled up the blinds to let the morning sun in through the bay windows of her rooftop turret. The paperboys slithered through the cracks of the neighbourhood's basin distributing today's news. WE ARE IN A STATE OF ALERT rang the headlines. 'Oh, the horror!' cried the lady as she met with the sax in the living room and switched on the television to learn of the latest developments. 'Threat levels are severe,' she repeated after the anchor. She rushed to her tablet and clutched it as she ran down the corridor opening the blinds on her way to the kitchen. The kettle whirred and the lady sought some solace in a cup of milky tea as she processed the following information: THE CURRENT THREAT LEVEL FOR INTERNATIONAL TERRORISM IS SEVERE.

The telephone rang. Dashing back across the apartment in the sky the lady grabbed the receiver at the third ring.

'Mornin' Marie,' came a laconic slur.

'Good morning, Karen,' replied the lady to the caretaker. 'Whatever is the matter at this early hour?'

Karen took a moment to reply and when she did she delivered the news with the stony steel of a cowboy assassin. 'It's Elizabeth. Down in flat number seven. The first floor. You know, Elizabeth, flat seven. Hello? Anyone ther—?'

'Yes yes I'm here Karen. Now please, spare me the suspense – what exactly is happening down in flat number seven?'

A pregnant pause presided. 'It's Nigel. He fell off his bed. Three o' clock in the morning. He's been on his back for four hours.'

Marie let out a delicate sigh of relief. Luckily her son was staying with her in the guest room. 'OK Karen I'll send Nico down post-haste.' And with that she went to knock on the guest room door only to find her eldest son awake, writing. 'Nico, darling, there is an emergency in flat number seven – Nigel's fallen agai—'

'I'm on it!' called Nico, already halfway down the stairwell, skipping over the aged green carpet in his slippers, taking two stairs at a time.

A sweet musk struck the tip of Nico's nose as he entered flat seven. Walls stacked with picture frames hung over ornaments of all shapes and sizes. As a bull in a china shop the young man darted through this labyrinth of objects to the bedroom where he found Nigel lying prone beneath his wife of many a decade at the foot of the bed.

'There he is Nico. He's all yours,' shrugged Karen, pointing at Nigel. The radio reported the details of an attack several neighbourhoods to the east: LATEST COUNT FOUR CONFIRMED DEAD TWENTY-ONE IN A CRITICAL CONDITION. COUNTLESS OTHERS INJURED, THOUGH THEY ARE SAID TO BE IN A STABLE STATE.

'Terrible, all of this, isn't it Nicholas?' chirped Nigel.

'It is,' replied the young man. 'Now let's get you back where you belong.' Nico scooched by Elizabeth and crouched behind her husband, gently sliding his hands past his shoulder blades and under his armpits until they rested where his forearms met his biceps on the underside of his elbows. He levered the old man gently though firmly through one hundred and eighty degrees of motion and laid him to rest at the head of the bed.

'The lad is strong,' wheezed Nigel and then he coughed and then he sneezed. 'You're a football player aren't you?'

Nico smiled at the old man who had decided he was a football player ever since he saw him kicking a ball around in the park across the road. 'That was almost ten years ago now!' replied Nico, as per usual, and with a hearty laugh to boot, also as per. 'Anyway, Nigel, you have a good day now. And you, Elizabeth, please call us at any hour of the night – I was wide awake at 3AM – you really needn't worry about the bother as there is none, my dear.'

Elizabeth rotated on her walking stick at snail's pace and looked up at him. 'Thank you, Nicholas,' she said.

It was clock-winding day at the apartment in the sky and Marie informed her son of this on his return through the front door, as she did every Thursday.

'Yes, mother, very good,' replied Nico.

Marie sat down at the desk and stared wistfully out towards the treetops of the park and wondered where the building was that always seemed to appear to her between the trees on Thursdays – clock-winding day. She soon accepted that she would never be able to work it out and turned to the clock, which was still as still could be. The morning light gleamed across its golden veneer and she smiled contentedly to herself as she swivelled the clock around one hundred and eighty degrees on the sun-stained tan brown leather surface of the desktop, and she wound the clock back up. The clock began to tick and tock and tick and tock and Marie smiled with glee. 'Oh, life! How I adore the sound of thee!' The drama of her day was over.

Meanwhile, deep inside the kingdom of the once-again-ticking clock, several neighbourhoods to the north of

Kristina's apartment, stood Layak in all of his morning glory. Thick globules of an inky pus-like substance were secreted by the pores where his stipe met his cup. He slid around the bathroom and whenever he tried to steady himself so that he could look at himself in the little round mirror hanging over that small square sink of his, he would fall back on his derrière right in the middle of the dung-covered floor tiles. 'I've got to get to work I can't keep missing days in the office because I've been playing the bugle with fucking Ben all night it's ridiculous fucking ridiculous look at the state I'm in for fuck's sake,' he yelped a-word-a-second. Finally, after many a tumble, Layak managed to grab on to the small square sink with the squid-like tentacles that had formed from the congealed ink-like substance that oozed out of every orifice. Heaving himself up with all of his might, this slippery, slimy mushroom headed fellow reached for the minuscule sack of brass nestled just under the mirror next to his razor and behind his toothbrush. 'Thank heavens!' he bellowed. 'Oh no!' he rasped. And he swallowed a thick globule of ink the size of a cantaloupe as he pulled the minuscule sack towards him with all of the courage he could muster.

Lying in the swamp that was his bathroom, Layak managed to meld a microscopic piece of brass with two other pieces, more microscopic still, into a bugle. 'It's small but it will do I can always go and get more brass there's a shop yes that new metal supermarket haven't you heard of it you know that one that's just opened around the corner may as well go there instead of to work. Work's a write-off mate!' Then, he tried to play the microscopic musical instrument he had fashioned. He pursed his lips with incredible force but his tongue was taut and would not cooperate with the rest of the muscles in his face. 'Who am I kidding?' he said to himself, resigned to his fate. 'I haven't had a job in a year and I have no prospects of getting another one in a state like this.' These were the first true words Layak had uttered to himself, or indeed to anyone for that matter, in the whole preceding year. It was in this

10

moment of truth that he forgot to breathe. The bumbling bandit started drowning in the rising swamp of his bathroom floor. 'Help!' he screamed. But it was no use. Layak swallowed a whole heap of dung and ink and any number of tiny bugle fragments and choked to death.

II

Brothers Wren

———

Cyril and Norfolk flitted about that neck of the woods with which you are by now somewhat familiar. But this pair of wrens was not the only source of sound slaloming through the vast skies of Kingdom Clock on this very morning. No. And in fact their ceaseless chirping was inaudible to most of the neighbourhood's residents at the birth of this mild summer's day. An alarm bell rang throughout the streets long since drained of the great floods and droned with a throbbing monotony. The bearded gentleman who liked to sit on the second bench of three in the winter garden, so named for its flowers that blossomed even during the darkest depths of a year's final season, would sit and read his newspapers which were all a high-brow-read or at the very least a mid-brow-read or at least he liked to think so, chewing on his cigar, sitting on his bench. WE ARE IN A STATE OF EMERGENCY barked one such paper. A Nation Weeps another. And just like this another day in the kingdom of the clock with a golden veneer grew into itself and its grasses gleamed with all that was gold.

There was, however, at least one lady in the neighbourhood who heard the songs of Cyril and Norfolk that morning and she awoke with a dainty yawn, her mouth mindfully guarded by her fingertips for the duration of this lapse. She eased out of bed and sloped towards the kitchen in search of coffee but was stopped in her tracks by the sight of two boxes nestled under the dining room table. 'Coffee comes first,' she thought. Yes, Kristina Ninotchka was not a lady to rush and this was particularly true on Sundays. Indeed on Sundays she displayed such stillness that time and space could barely be perceived by anyone who should try. Moreover, Ms Ninotchka was a lady of such elegance that this too was barely perceived by the many she would pass by over the course of her days and I note that such elegance may sound like an exaggeration on behalf of this narrator. But I will hear nothing of it! Believe it or not, Kristina Ninotchka was a lady of unfathomable grace too. She also had her priorities and today these consisted of coffee and two boxes in that order.

Perched on an upturned wicker basket, Kristina admired the many shades of green and ensconced herself in them. She moved her lips to her coffee and with it she wetted them and it was then that she heard the chirping. 'That sounds like Cyril,' she thought. 'And that's Norfolk,' she said. 'Yes, Cyril and Norfolk are here today.' And with that she set down her cup of coffee beside her on the wicker basket and left it there as she made for the kitchen once again. The brothers Wren were in fact perched on a knobbly branch of a vine that crawled up the worn red brick of this distinguished lady's block. There they sat among the leaves each of them no larger than the lady's littlest fingers.

On this morning the brothers discussed greatness as was their custom on Sundays. 'Lord Fedra is the greatest super hero of them all,' began Cyril 'and I shall tell you why, my dearest brother.'

Norfolk relaxed his little feathery chest and gazed out into the winter garden poised to chime in as and when it was time to do so.

'Now, when the Fedra raises his axe above his heads, there is simply no telling when he will bring it down over the neck of his victim.'

This was true, thought Norfolk, so he allowed his brother to continue.

'To wield a weapon of the greatest strength is to wield it with the softest of touches, yet, at the same time, the most incisive of motions and the most brutal of forces.'

Norfolk was now moved to speak. 'I agree, my brother, save for one small detail,' he chirped.

13

'Do go on,' replied Cyril.

'Superheroes are timeless.'

And at that moment Kristina Ninotchka returned with her hands raised and cupped and carrying two tiny treats for the brothers Wren. Among the crevices of her palms nestled the most minuscule of porcelain cups, of which there were two, one for Cyril and the other for Norfolk. The birds flapped their wings gently and flew down into her hands and jumped up and down two times each, though not at the same time, to show their appreciation for Kristina Ninotchka, who smiled at them with her cherry-shaped eyes. 'The tea with milk and molasses is for you Cyril. The oatmeal and molasses is for you Norfolk. Enjoy.' And it was in this moment that the birds took the tiny porcelain cups in their wings and admired them in their grasp. The cups were adorned by blue sunflowers painted by Kristina herself.

'These are new,' chirped Cyril.

'Yes. The painting is anyway,' she replied. 'I completed them yesterday evening at sundown.'

'Delicious oats,' chimed Norfolk already halfway through the portion.

'You're a hungry little one, aren't you, dearest Norfolk,' Kristina acknowledged with a smile. 'Now, where were we boys? The Fedra, I believe.' And she sat back down on her wicker basket and moved her coffee to her lips and wetted them once more as the birds continued tweeting about greatness for several moments more.

A blackbird swooped down and rested on the wrought iron railing of the balcony. 'I beg to differ!' he squawked, bringing the conversation about greatness to a halt until he segued seamlessly into a suggestion of his own: 'Zenus Zanus is in fact the greatest super hero of them all,' he crowed and with complete and utter conviction in the truth of his statement did he crow. Cyril and Norfolk were accustomed to greeting the suggestions of outsiders with levity for their meditations on the matter of greatness had spanned their entire lives

14

together and the lore was deep – it is true! But the sheer control with which the blackbird delivered his words resonated deeply within their little feathery bodies. 'The head of Zenus is made of stone so hard that nothing and no one has ever survived contact with it.'

Cyril nodded but he was not totally convinced and he probed, 'With what regularity does Zanus of Zenus wield this weapon for I can only remember him doing so once' – and then Norfolk chimed, 'Twice.'

Then, in this very moment, the blackbird stood over the wrens and just when they least expected it, he replied. 'Exactly.'

'Who are you?' asked Norfolk of the blackbird.

'I am Benjamin,' he responded without a semblance of hesitation. 'Benjamin, the bugle-playing-blackbird.' And with that the newest member of the group retrieved a bugle from under his wing that was so small that it defied all of the laws of the most contemporary of physical theories and even Kristina Ninotchka, she of the utmost stillness and elegance and grace, blushed.

In the winter garden the trees' leaves rustled in the soft summer winds and Norfolk marvelled at the ripening peaches of one particular tree. 'Life pulses through these golden peaches,' he said and then he thought that they would make delicious jam. 'I must leave now, Ms Ninotchka,' he turned and said to her. 'Thank you for breakfast.' And with that Norfolk flew towards that tiny tree resplendent in a golden dress made entirely of a thousand shimmering peaches – their skin so shiny and taut – and he took one in his beak to make into jam for tea.

'Is that your brother?' asked Benjamin of Cyril.

'Yes he is and a very special bird he is too,' came the reply.

Kristina Ninotchka ushered Benjamin the blackbird and Cyril the wren indoors and to the dining room table. 'I need your help,' she said to them and she flew under the table and retrieved two caramel-coloured and cube-shaped cardboard boxes from underneath. 'This afternoon we shall build a ship,' she said. Setting them down on the table she opened them both and gazed at the contents with love and she turned to Benjamin and gave to him a tiny piece of moss-covered bark. The moss had hardened in the summer's sun and was almost prickly to the touch.

'All shades of green ever seen in all the vast expanses of Kingdom Clock reside on this tiny piece of bark,' said Benjamin the blackbird.

'Yes, dearest Benjamin, each and every one of them. It shall be your job to construct the ship from this piece of bark and you shall use these tools to do so,' and with that she retrieved the tiniest of tiny toolboxes from that same caramel-coloured box from which she had retrieved the tiny piece of bark. 'And Cyril – surely you know what I shall ask of you, dearest friend.' And with that Cyril relaxed his feathery stomach and flapped his little wings and floated over the dining room table to the second of the two caramel-coloured and cube-shaped cardboard boxes. He hopped all over the box and pecked at it until all that one could see was a multitude, nay, a myriad of minuscule objects, from pencils and rulers to leather-clad juggling balls and dictionaries. 'Once the ship is complete, you will arrange all of these minuscule items within it.'

Benjamin wore a bemused expression on his pitch-black face. 'Why?' he crowed.

Kristina Ninotchka smiled. 'So that each and every item will be accessible to us without thought of where it may be stored throughout our voyage. This will save us time on our journey so that we can enjoy the scenery as we sail,' she said.

No time had passed when the ship was ready to sail and the blackbird and the wren worked together to knit a net that fitted the ship like a glove. The net had two small pieces of the smallest rope one could imagine loose at either end of this hammock-like net and the birds lowered the ship into it. Kristina flew onto the deck and the birds carried her on this ship that sat snuggly in this net and with the smallest rope one could imagine held tightly in their smallest of beaks. And just like this they flew the lady to the lake in the park where their voyage would begin. Throughout that mild summer's afternoon they sailed.

'Bit breezy,' said Benjamin.

'I like it,' chirped Cyril.

And Kristina Ninotchka gazed out at the sunny haze emanating from the ruby red reeds that waved in the wind throughout this stunningly still lake.

The sun was setting and the birds sat together at the bow of the ship. Cyril had been charged with plotting their path as per usual and he flitted between the handles of the maroon-coloured mahogany wheel with the feathery feel of a bird well acquainted with such a task. 'Thank you, dearest Cyril,' the lady would whisper whenever he made an adjustment to their course through the ruby red reeds of the lake. All the while Benjamin the blackbird played a myriad of beautifully crafted brass instruments and Kristina Ninotchka was awe-struck. 'So it is not just the bugle that you play!' The blackbird played and the wren steered and the lady laughed with all that was lovely in the kingdom of the clock with the golden veneer.

III

The Tin Din

―――

TIN DIN flashed a red neon light bearing the name of a haunted restaurant. It was Friday night and as the clock struck twelve this deepest darkest pocket of Kingdom Clock rocked with all manner of mayhem. This neighbourhood lay in the basement of the ticking clock, shielded by a thin sheet of tin that obscured it from the rest of the neighbourhoods in the kingdom. Though this enclave was seldom silent, tonight was a particularly raucous affair and everyone was hellbent on marching to the beat of their own drum. Amidst the chaos of the din an ageing hyena sat slumped on the extractor fan outside the front door. He played a self-made bugle in a herky-jerky manner and hatched a most devilish plan. This ageing hyena was known to have a grand plan or two and indeed he had had many a plan in his time. Nothing, though, was quite as ambitious as the idea he pondered that Friday night, slumped outside of his restaurant tucked away in the deepest recesses of the ticking clock.

curtain raises

ELLIOT   The one thing this place needs is a piano.
MIKE   I'm so sorry Elliot, would you be a dear and repeat that please?
ELLIOT   A piano! This place needs one – don'tcha reckon mate?
MIKE   That's a very good idea indeed mate!
ELLIOT   Thanks Mikey, I knew you'd be on board …
MIKE   Tip top plan, love it!

Mike the meerkat turned back to the big book and filled out the final row of numbers for the day and shut it closed. The book read ACCOUNTS.

MIKE   'Ow are we going to get it through the front door tho' Ell?

ELLIOT   You know what Mikey – I 'adn't thought that far ahead! *laughs*

MIKE   Don't worry mate, we'll figure somethin' out.

ELLIOT   We always do, mate. We always do.

MIKE   Very true, Ell, we do indeed! Anyway, you got any plans for the rest of the evenin'?

ELLIOT   Well as a matter of fact I do! There's a lovely young bitch awaiting my call across town. Don't know if I can be fucked though to be honest with ya mate. She's a fruit loop.

MIKE   Is that the spotted hyena you mentioned the other day?

ELLIOT   Yeah, that's the one.

MIKE   What's her name again?

ELLIOT   Don't ask me mate! *cackles*

MIKE   *chuckles*

And with that Mike and Elliot left the office in the basement of the TIN DIN and scampered up the stairs and out the front door of the restaurant.

MIKE   Oh no mate!

ELLIOT   What's that mate?

MIKE   The lock's broken!

ELLIOT   What do you mean the lock's broken?

MIKE   I mean I can't lock the restaurant door.

ELLIOT   Oh. Well, never mind mate, there's nothin' in there anyway.

MIKE   Very true mate.

And just like that another day at the TIN DIN drew to a close and the meerkat and the hyena scampered through the alleyways of town playing their fiddles on each and every street corner en route home.

**

The clock struck twelve on Saturday night and We Can Be Heroes Just for One Day blared out through the hubbub of the neighbourhood. TIN DIN flickered and threatened to stop illuminating the restaurant entirely, though it never went out for long enough to spark concern. Scampering back and forth through the flickering neon of the neighbourhood's trash-ridden alleyways were Bob the badger and Florence the fox.

BOB	I found it! I knew there'd be one here somewhere!
FLORENCE	What did you find bobby brown eyes?
BOB	There's always at least one here – standard procedure.
FLORENCE	What's the standard procedure brown eyes?
BOB	You're a dickhead if you don't know that by now quite frankly.
FLORENCE	You're being MEAN brown eyes! Why do you always have to be so MEAN!
BOB	Go and die in that steaming pile of trash over there you filthy whore.
FLORENCE	NO! BROWN EYES! STOP IT! YOU'RE GONNA MAKE ME—
BOB	Cry?
FLORENCE	*wails uncontrollably*
BOB	Good grief – you're a liability – you're going to get us caught you fucking tramp.
FLORENCE	*regains composure* At least I'm a hot tramp bobby brown eyes …
BOB	I'll grant you that.

Sirens rang through the tempestuous backstreets of this haunted neighbourhood and alleycats meowed with all of their mighty little lungs and Bob chased Florence and Florence chased Bob until finally they rested in a cosy can of trash.

BOB   Good call on this can Flo – nice change of scenery.
FLO   It's a nice nest in which to rest bobby brown eyes.
BOB   Stop calling me brown eyes stupid bitch!
FLO   No! YOU stop it!
BOB   Stop what?
FLO   Being mean.

police sirens

BOB   Speak up love I can't hear you.
FLO   STOP BEING MEAN.

sound of sirens ratchets up

BOB   You what love?
FLO   STOP. BEING. MEEEAAAN!
BOB   What?
FLO   MEEEEEEAAAAAAN!
BOB   WHAT?
FLO   *wails uncontrollably*
BOB   Goodness gracious me, you're a mess Flo.
FLO   *regains composure* We're both a mess bobby brown eyes.
BOB   Well that's something we can agree on at least.
FLO   Finally!

And with that the fox and the badger roughed and tumbled and took turns playing an old trombone in the trash can through the night and at daybreak they drifted off in each other's arms to a gentle slumber.

**

It was midday in the neighbourhood and TIN DIN glistened in the aftermath of the storm. Joey jumped and skipped through the potholes and puddles – today was his time to shine! A lone wolf, Joey was magnificent and mellow in equal measure. He loved the TIN DIN dearly and on Sundays it was his own. His golden coat shimmered in the midday sun and upon reaching the door to the restaurant he noticed it was ajar and the lock broken.

JOEY   What the fuck man! What in the bleeding HELL is going on!

He howled at the top of his lungs and his howling reverberated through this sleepy neighbourhood in the tin-covered base of the clock with the golden veneer.

JOEY   I've gotta just take five and calm down for a second.

And so the wolf of the golden coat resplendent in the midday sun found a shady spot in the alleyway behind the restaurant and dived into the dustbin where he stored his wares. All manner of materials gleamed before him. There were all of the staples – brass and aluminium among them; the precious metals – gold, silver and bronze. Then there was the toolbox in which he stored those things needed to conjoin the metals – a soldering iron the most important of them all.

JOEY   Aight let's get to work!

And the din that the young wolf made was quite spectacular and it rang throughout the neighbourhood and jigged and shrieked among the puddles and the potholes.

drilling

A policeman walked over to the trash can and peered into its depths.

POLICEMAN   Well, well, well – what 'av we going on 'ere then?
JOEY   I'm making a French horn, my brother! What brings you to my workshop?
POLICEMAN   Well, young wolf, I'm here to inform you that the lock on TIN DIN is broken.
JOEY   Yeah bruv, I know. I'm gonna get to that when I'm done with the horn.
POLICEMAN   Well, I suppose everything is alright then. Never mind me!
JOEY   See ya bro.
POLICEMAN   I'll be seeing you then.

soldering and drilling reach fever pitch

Soon enough the French horn was complete and it was truly a sight to behold only matched by the beauty with which Joey played it.

drilling abates

JOEY   Right, time to get to work. Let's start with the agenda …

Behind the bar lay a post-it affixed to the greasy almond-coloured countertop.

JOEY   People have got to start cleaning this place – what the fuck! MAN.

The following note had been left for Joey by the previous evening's manager, in this case Mike.

DEAREST JOEY

HERE IS THE AGENDA FOR SUNDAY

3PM   TRIAL SHIFT OF MARC THE MOUSE
5PM   ELL ARRIVES FOR STOCKCHECK
7PM   I ARRIVE FOR DINNER SERVICE
9PM   CLOSE EARLY TO INSTALL GRAND PIANO

KIND REGARDS

MIKE

PS FLORENCE AND BOB ARE GOING TO POP BY TO HELP US CARRY THE PIANO FROM VIKING STREET OVER TO THE RESTAURANT

JOEY   Today's gonna be a good day – I can feel it!

And he poured himself a glass of apple juice and took it outside to the extractor fan where he sipped it and played his French horn in the afternoon sun.

***

The clock struck three and the most mini of all the mice awoke from his stony slumber in a quite sophisticated neighbourhood of Kingdom Clock. Cafés sparkled with the signs and sounds of the glitterati sipping their lazy Sunday coffees. All manner of languages melded together as one and the scents of the finest cuisines in all of the kingdom of the clock with the golden veneer sang together as one.

MARC Oh no! It's already 3PM! I'm going to be late for my
      trial shift!

And with that he raced through the neighbourhood and then
the next one and then another one still, snacking on the vast
array of golden crumbs that had fallen from the glistening
tables of the glitterati, until he reached TIN DIN.

MARC Sorry I'm late! It's not normal for me to be late! I
      promise!
JOEY WHAT.
MARC I was due at 3PM for my trial shift!
JOEY OH. You must be Marc the mouse.
MARC Yes that's me! It's 1501 and I was due at 1500! I'm so
      very so—
JOEY SHUT UP.
MARC *embarrassed*

And that was how Marc the mouse and Joey the wolf of the
glimmering golden coat became acquainted. Throughout that
lazy late afternoon shift, Joey taught Marc everything he knew
about precious metals, playing the horn and the deepest
darkest lore of TIN DIN.

MARC Wow! It's really like that here!?
JOEY Yes, my brother. It's really like that here – and you're
      gonna fit it just fine.
MARC Really!?
JOEY Yes, my brother. Just you wait and see.

And just like that Elliot made his appearance onstage.

ELLIOT YES MATE.
JOEY   YES ELLIE!
ELLIE   What you saying Jo?

JO	Not much, my brother, just showing little Marc here the ropes.
ELLIE	Who's Marc?
JO	The mouse right here of course!

And standing and trembling beneath and between Jo and Ellie was indeed Marc the most mini of all of the mice in the kingdom of the clock with the golden veneer.

MARC	Hi! Down here!
ELLIE	Oh. Hi there lil' guy. Pleased to meet you.
JO	He's got a great work ethic, my brother.
ELLIE	Is that so?
JO	Yes mate. He cleaned the entire restaurant in an hour and we've just been jammin' for the last hour or so. He's. A. Fucking. LEGEND.
ELLIE	It is very fresh and clean in here, I must say!
JO	L-L-LEGEND!
ELLIE	L-L-LEGEND is right … This is the cleanest the place has been in a decade!

And so Ellie and Jo conspired to stock the fridges with bottled bugles of all shapes and sizes, testing them out as they went. Meanwhile, Marc sat atop a tiny little round wooden stall with the longest of legs and nibbled at the delightful delicacies of the TIN DIN.

MARC	This is great! I haven't eaten like this in ages! Thank you so much guys!
JO	You love it here already don't you my brother?
MARC	It's true! I do! Oh, I do, IT'S TRUE.
ELLIE	That's the spirit Marky! TRUTH.
JO	T-T-TRUTH.
MARKY	T-T-TRUTH!

And so Jo, he of the magnificent golden coat, ventured out through the rains of the early evening to his sheltered spot in the back alley behind TIN DIN. He jumped into the trash can and rummaged through his wares and made a magnificent trumpet – oh, it truly was magnificent, this narrator assures you! In actual fact, he made three! And the wolf and the hyena and lil' Marky the mouse formed a band and played the trumpet to their hearts' content. The clock struck seven and Mike entered the fray to the tune of The Man Who Sold the World.

MIKE	Evening gents – how are we?
ELLIE & JO	Tip top, thank you very much, mate!
MIKE	And who's this lil' fella?
MARKY	I'm Marky! I bring TRUTH!
ELLIE & JO	T-T-TRUTH!
MIKE	You bring truth, huh. Well that's much needed about these parts, so thank you, Marky.
MARKY	It's nothing at all! The truth is Mr Mike, sir, I've never felt so accepted anywhere in my whole entire life! I truly feel I've united with a band of long-lost brothers!
MIKE	That's music to my ears fella – you're going to love working here, I'm sure of it.

And with that Mike managed the dinner session with the utmost competence and grace. His composure permeated TIN DIN and for once, it didn't seem like such a chaotic hellhole after all. C-C-CHANGES rang through the restaurant and all of the animals of KINGDOM CLOCK dined and laughed and cherish the precious moment together, as one.

MIKE	Right, time to wrap this up. Boys, I'm going outside to play my fiddle and touch up the paint on the facade. Tonight it shall be painted gold.
AS ONE	TIP TOP.

When Mike had finished painting he returned to the fray once more and the final customers made their way for the exit. Jo locked the door, which he had constructed from solid gold to match Mike's choice for the colour of the facade. Florence and Bob turned up and knocked on the door and Marc dashed across the gleaming wooden floors, which he had varnished in the afternoon, and scuttled up the door to unlock it.

MARC   Hi guys! Great to see you! Come join us at the island! We're playing the bugle!

FLO & BOB B-B-BUGLES.

And just like that Mike and Elliot and Joey and Marc and Florence and Bob sat on the island and discussed whether there was Life on Mars.

ELLIOT   There's a star man in the sky – I know that much!

JOEY   True that, my brother, there most certainly is.

MIKE   Ya reckon?

BOB   Nah, just the moon man at this hour.

MARC   MOON.

FLO   M-M-MOON.

ALL AS ONE M-M-MOOOOOON!

Now, there was one more task on the agenda for the band before they could get too comfortable and Mike informed them of the plan.

MIKE We'll just have to pop over to Viking Street to pick up the grand piano.

BOB The what?

ELLIOT We're removing this here island and replacing it with a grand piano.

MARC That's a great idea!

FLO   Oh, lil' Marc – you have blue eyes!
MARC   *blushes*

The band marched through the streets of this neon-clad neighbourhood in the depths of the kingdom of the clock with the golden veneer and worked as a team through the night. When Monday morning came the grand piano ushered in the week playing itself so sweetly that the streets would glitter with all that was gold through another working week.

curtain falls

IV

War

———

a pigeon sat in his coop

caw caw

the war was over

caw caw

and babylon had been razed to the ground

caw caw

only cockroaches walked the kingdom of the clock

and a solitary pigeon who sat in his coop

caw caw

this pigeon was lucky to have a safe spot to reside in

he looked about his coop

caw caw

there was nothing save a solitary plastic bag from waitrose

the only store to survive the war

caw caw

in this bag were the keys to the coop and everything else he owned including a two pound coin and perhaps a twenty pence piece or so

caw caw

the pigeon sat and protected his plastic bag which contained each and every little thing that he owned

caw caw

he no longer owned a phone

caw caw

all of the screens in the kingdom of the clock had been smashed into a thousand little pieces and fragments lay in every nook and cranny of the kingdom

caw caw

but they did not gleam

caw caw

instead they shone with all the shine of coal

caw caw

the pigeon did not speak

caw caw

he had forgotten how to

but that was ok because he still had his centre

caw caw

and his appetites

caw caw

touched by thirst he flew slowly towards the bag which hung
from the ceiling where the lampshade used to shield him and
his friends from the glare of the bulb and protected them
from its brightness through many a party

caw caw

but this pigeon had forgotten all about those parties and
those days when he and his friends would play all manner of
musical instruments together in the coop

caw caw

now it was silent

caw caw

he was still

caw

and he flew up to retrieve the bottle of lipton iced tea

caw

lemon

caw

my favourite

caw

but now only one drop remained

caw caw

and the pigeon consumed that final drop

and the raven banged against the coop

caw

the pigeon was still

caw

he was still

V

SITTING UNDER A TREE

IN THE WINTER

GARDEN

I PROPOSE TO THEE

TO LEAVE

THIS GREAT CITY

AND RETIRE TO

A LAND MORE APT FOR ME

WHERE THE WEATHER

DOES NOT DITHER

AND COMMITS

TO ITS GOAL

OF NOURISHING

THEE

AND I WILL SING & DANCE

AND WRITE & PRANCE

AND GENERALLY

I WILL ACT THE FOOL

AND WHEN THE VALLEY

FILLS TO ITS BRIM

AND BECOMES A GIANT POOL

I PROPOSE TO THEE

OH, KRISTINA

NINOTCHKA

MARRY ME

VI

skipping and vaulting

hazy mazy fields liaise

a super hero

VII

Soul Sweeper

———

A worn soul swept the restaurant floor at the end of the day. This activity consumed every last sinew of Mi Na's body. He dashed about the space, back and forth, until it was spotless and then he mopped with greater will still. When it was time to lock up, the urge to leave was so strong that simply turning the key and stepping outside the front door did nothing to relieve him. He stood waiting to be washed by a wave of euphoria but it did not come. Alarmed, he unlocked the door and went back inside the restaurant to clean it all over again. But no matter how much he cleaned he was not pricked even by the edge of enthusiasm. 'I must leave now,' he thought. 'The restaurant, this town and everybody in it. I must go to a place far away, where sweeping and mopping are a distant memory.' Opportunity, faith and love had fallen by the wayside and it was the end of this journey to recapture them to a degree more pure than ever before. He slept soundly that night, dreaming of a tropical island thick with jungle, its inhabitants going about their daily lives where the lush trees parted and made way to expanses of sandy beaches.

The morning sun rose and he informed his deputy of the plan, who greeted the idea with confusion and contempt. Failing to dissuade Mi Na, he finally conceded that this was a necessary venture.

'When will you return?' he asked.

Soon, not-for-a-while and never became one in Mi Na's mind. 'I don't know,' he said.

By midday he had informed each and every one of those close to him of his decision. His mother was anxious and warned of the dangers ahead, his brother dismayed and his lover heartbroken. Numb to all of this, Mi Na sought a semblance of calm in the few possessions he packed in a small leather bag. Among an assortment of clothes, each item rolled up into a ball no larger than a fist, nestled a small book containing the writings of a monk. 'I will understand these words,' he said to himself. 'To observe nature and describe it so plainly as to capture all of life's wonders at once. How such insight dangles over my poor head as a low-hanging fruit bobbing stubbornly beyond my grasp!'

A train pulled into the station and Mi Na travelled south through the countryside. The sun's rays sparkled among the flooded paddy fields and the young man felt sure that this was the most beautiful moment to which he had ever been privy. He retrieved a pen and notebook from his bag and pondered the disconnect between his life at home and the harmony of the elements with the farmland. 'A sodden field owes its fate to the rains, to no man does it yield, this sodden field.' Pained by the trite nature of his words he punished himself by thinking of nothing but nothingness for the rest of the ride. Even this was no mean feat. Mi Na grappled with rushing thoughts about man's neglect of nature, flooding and the miraculous properties of skin until his head finally fell into his lap.

The train driver woke Mi Na at the end of the line. The terminus stood on a hill that overlooked a turquoise sea and a small harbour of exactly one boat. 'Hurry and you will make the next trip out to the island!' called the driver. Mi Na held his bag to his chest and ran down the hill as quickly as his legs could carry him. At the base of the hill lay a creaking wooden boardwalk where fishermen smoked. 'Please come along now,' said a boatman. Mi Na thanked him and climbed aboard.

Sacks of rice sat in the bay of the boat and a disparate band of travellers gathered around them. Some turned to the sea and others to their comrades but Mi Na was transfixed by the sacks of rice. 'The poetry lies in the process,' he thought. 'What are the paddy fields and the farmers without the sacks and the boats and the boatmen?' A seagull circled the boat and came to rest on the bow. She stood with such poise that no one aboard could fail to notice. Even the boatmen saluted the bird as she flew between the rice sacks and inspected them one by one to rapturous applause. When she was done, she flew to the stern and stayed there for the duration of the ride.

Longtail boats anchored at the shore cast their evening shadows and fluffy clouds danced with the evening sun over the sea. The boat was tied up and everyone disembarked. No sooner had Mi Na felt the sand between his toes than a young boy cried out to him – 'Hey you!' Startled, Mi Na realised that he had forgotten how to speak on the voyage. 'Do you want fried noodles or noodle soup?' Mi Na repeated the words noodle and soup after the boy. 'Do you want chicken or pork or beef?' Pork, please. 'Do you want water or cola or iced coffee?' Water, please. 'Please take a seat.'

It was only then that Mi Na noticed three benches lined up on the beach. A single space remained on the middle one. With the words noodle and soup and pork and water rattling around in his ears Mi Na observed the boy. 'Never have I seen such a command of a restaurant,' he thought. Remembering his own restaurant he shook his head in shame. 'It is true that this boy only offers two dishes, which are practically the same, and that three benches is a small capacity, but never mind it! He is working alone and cannot be more than eight years old.' Chicken or pork or beef and water or cola or iced coffee became all that Mi Na knew. The boy ran up to the cauldron of steaming noodles stirred dutifully by his mother and back to the benches relaying bowl after bowl of fried noodles and noodle soup with chicken or pork or beef. Carrying the drinks was so effortless for the boy that he skipped between tables and climbed among customers to give them water or cola or iced coffee. The food was delicious. Mi Na chewed up the noodles and slurped down the soup almost as soon as the glorious scent had wafted under his nostrils.

'Three dollar fifty, please.' The boy stood still and smiled sweetly.

'The humility of this child is unlike anything I have ever seen,' thought Mi Na. 'I must reward him at once!' And so he handed over a five dollar bill and explained that the change was for him and his mother. The boy shrieked with delight and made for his mother's arms, who cradled her son with boundless joy.

That evening the island cooled and Mi Na found a hut to rest in by sundown. All manner of creatures knocked about in the rickety old hut from bugs and rats to lizards and bats and this continued through the night. Despite the cacophony of jungle noise surrounding Mi Na he could not hear any of it. All he could think of was the boy. 'To call him a boy would be to pay him a disservice. He is an adult in any meaningful sense of the word. He runs his restaurant with consummate skill. How can one achieve this level of professionalism at such an age? Love. Love is the only conceivable answer.' With that thought, Mi Na decided that he would eat fried noodles in the morning and noodle soup in the evening as long as he remained on the island. Each time the boy would command his space with greater authority. One time he apologised for the chickens had not yet been killed that day. Another time he berated a fully grown man for killing a chicken in the wrong way. 'Not like that! Like this!' he would shout.

The man appeared to be the boy's father and one morning Mi Na decided to introduce himself.

'Hello, sir,' he said to the man.

'Hello,' the man replied.

'Your boy is one of a kind.'

At this the man recoiled and revealed a toothy grin. 'Thank you for your help,' he said.

Mi Na explained that he was the one who should be

grateful, for the man's boy had inspired him and made his journey worthwhile.

'Thank you for your help,' the man repeated.

'What is his name?' Mi Na asked.

'Su Rong.'

Mi Na ate his noodles and Su Rong appeared before him when the bowl was empty. 'Three dollar fifty, please,' he stated, like clockwork.

Checking his pockets, it occurred to Mi Na that on this occasion he only had three dollars and fifty cents to offer the boy. He acknowledged that his tipping had become customary and so he broke it to him as gently as he could – 'No tip this morning, double tip this evening.'

At that Su Rong let out a primordial scream and sobbed to his heart's content. His veneer of composure par excellence had been shattered into a thousand irreconcilable pieces.

'I must leave now,' thought Mi Na. Numbed once more he packed his bag, locked his hut and boarded the next boat back to the mainland. He did not marvel at the sacks of rice, nor did he wonder at a seagull. Instead he mulled over the illusion of purity that had been wrested from him. 'The island was a mistake but I cannot return to sweeping. My soul cannot sweep any longer. I must continue this venture.' The train was waiting at the station when the boat pulled into the harbour on the mainland. Mi Na held his bag to his chest and ran up the hill as fast as his legs could carry him. He boarded the train and travelled north through the countryside. 'To the mountains,' he said to himself. 'That is where truth can be found.'

The train pulled up at the northernmost stop. At this juncture in the valley the milky brown river flowed slowly. 'This evening will be devoid of cool air,' said Mi Na to himself. 'Perhaps there will be some freshness in the deep of the night.' This time he did not concern himself with finding a hut before dark. Walking along the riverbank, he circled the village again and again. 'He walked alone through the night, seeking fresh air with all of his might.' Mi Na was bothered by the ordinariness of his poetry but he would not punish himself for it. 'The river moves slowly but it will make it to the sea,' he pondered. Once he had been able to inhale a breath of fresh air he found a hut to stay in by midnight. Off the beaten track this hut was part of a small cluster. A swing swayed in a courtyard decorated with potted plants and covered by palm trees. Mi Na rested on the swing and just when he was on the verge of drifting away he was greeted by a young man about his own age.

'Hello, I am Xeng Xong, the caretaker. Could I take your bag and bring you coffee?' In no mood to sleep, Mi Na accepted the offer of coffee but insisted he carry his own bag. Xeng Xong smiled sweetly and showed his guest to his hut.

Sitting on the edge of the bed, Mi Na rambled to himself, 'Beware of those with sweet smiles singing songs about coffee, he'd better not be wretched too lest I feel the urge to flee . . .'

Xeng Xong knocked on the door. 'Please come in,' Mi Na called. The caretaker gestured to his guest to join him in the courtyard. The coffee was ready. The pair of them sat on the swing and let it sway slowly back and forth.

After several minutes of silence Xeng Xong was moved to speak. 'Please teach me,' he said in a hushed tone.

'There is nothing I can teach you,' replied Mi Na wearily.

'Teach me to speak like you.'

As far as Mi Na could tell, Xeng Xong was able to articulate everything he needed to. 'You already speak like I do.'

Xeng Xong hunched over and stared at his hands. 'I can speak to guests when they arrive and leave. I can take your bag and bring you coffee. But that is all.' Looking over at him Mi Na noticed that Xeng Xong had exceptionally large hands for a man of his size. He was short and lean. 'My hands are the hands of my father,' he said.

'Are you from the mountains?' This was the first statement to evade Xeng Xong's comprehension. It was then that Mi Na became captivated once more. 'I must be understood by this young man – this good man! All he has done is what I have asked, yet here I sit assuming the futility of it all. But why? This malaise has been brought on by a worthless setback. No – fatigue is the culprit! Well, the coffee is kicking in, so let's do this!'

Xeng Xong and Mi Na stayed up all night talking to each other about the worlds they had left behind to meet that night in the courtyard. Setting off long before sunrise, Xeng Xong would say good bye to his parents and trek down towards the valley. On his way he would practise mental arithmetic and ponder the questions of science. School ran from sunrise till mid-afternoon. Then he would swim in the river with his classmates and take a meal before crossing the village for the night shift at the inn.

'But the river is muddy,' noted Mi Na.

'Some parts are clear.'

Mi Na wondered how the river was affected by the seasons but Xeng Xong did not understand what he meant by this.

'Well, I am from a town on the other side of the mountains. There, we have four phases of weather each year.'

This seemed impossible to Xeng Xong, who proclaimed, 'There is a rainy season and there is a sunny season.' It was true. Rain and sun are pretty much ubiquitous on this planet of ours.

'But,' continued Mi Na, 'where I'm from we have a snowy season and a season when the leaves of the trees turn from green to brown.'

This astonished Xeng Xong. He had heard of snow and the process of water turning to ice at freezing temperatures was familiar to him from his studies. But green leaves turning brown? This was beyond his understanding. Mi Na explained that the tree itself does not die when this happens. 'Only the leaves die?' asked Xeng Xong. Mi Na smiled.

'Yes, just like hair that falls out of your head.'

As the days passed the young men bonded over their diverse backgrounds. Mi Na dazzled Xeng Xong with tales of cities comprising millions of citizens. The sheer number of zeroes, all six of them and sometimes seven, made Xeng Xong smile a great deal. When he found out that there was a country, nay two countries, each playing host to over a billion people, he was blown away by a crescendo of hearty laughter.

'But what of your home?' Mi Na asked. 'How is it there?'

Xeng Xong slumped back on the swing. 'When my mother falls ill, my father sacrifices a chicken. When my father falls ill, my mother sacrifices another chicken. Many chickens die like this where I am from.'

Mi Na wondered what his friend thought of this purported correlation.

'We get better after the chicken is sacrificed but I think we would get better anyway,' Xeng Xong pondered.

'It is a tradition,' thought Mi Na. 'We have traditions too,' he said. 'Where I'm from,' he began, 'we ask ourselves why.'

Xeng Xong did not understand. 'Why?' he repeated.

'Yes, why. Why are we here? What is the purpose for all of this?'

Xeng Xong's confusion showed no sign of abating.

'Put it this way,' Mi Na continued. 'The sun causes heat. It is the reason plants and trees grow. You could say that the sun is why we are here.' Xeng Xong nodded attentively. 'Now, given this, I put to you, Xeng Xong of the mountains, why are we here?'

After a moment's pause he replied, 'I am here because of my mother and father.' He was correct. His mother and father were indeed his reason to be.

'But what of them?' Mi Na pressed on.

'My mother is here because of her mother and father and my father is here because of his mother and father,' Xeng Xong reasoned.

'Yes! But what of their mothers and fathers?' The men gave each other a knowing look and laughed wildly all at once.

Then a serious expression painted itself over Xeng Xong's face. 'We come from monkeys,' he concluded.

Mi Na felt like he had been punched squarely between the eyes but adrenaline coursed through him and he felt nothing. 'Did you learn that at school?' he asked.

'No,' replied Xeng Xong.

That night Mi Na lay on his back in bed. The sounds of wildlife around him passed through him as one. 'Xeng Xong is a phenomenon,' he thought. 'He deduced the theory of evolution as though it were a matter of pure logic, though I'm sure his exposure to a multitude of animals has something to do with it. Regardless! I am sated at last. I shall reside at this inn till the end of my days and teach Xeng Xong everything I know. He does not even demand a cent for my wisdom. Oh, how much more pure could an exchange be than one in which money does not change hands!'

Mi Na awoke to the sound of clucking hens. He spent his day as he had become accustomed to, walking alongside the milky brown river, circling the village again and again until the deep of the night, for which he waited with bated breath. When it was cool enough to inhale the succulent night air without inhibition, he returned to the courtyard to meet with Xeng Xong.

Tonight, however, the caretaker had changed his tune. 'What business do you do in your town?' he asked.

Mi Na told him that he had a restaurant and that he was enjoying some time away from the place. It was in good hands.

'You make money in the big town from the restaurant business. Here, there is no money. I learn math and science at school. I learn to speak better with you. All of my friends do something like this. But in the end we are poor and the government is rich. Why?' Xeng Xong launched that why deep into Mi Na's heart with all of the skill of someone who had wielded that weapon his whole life.

'That is a very big why!'

'Why?' the caretaker repeated. Mi Na went to great lengths to explain supply and demand and capitalism and socialism and corruption and justice and good and evil but none of this satisfied Xeng Xong. 'Why?' he repeated.

'I'm sorry, I have no answer for you,' Mi Na replied. From that moment onwards the men would no longer speak as equals. Xeng Xong insisted that he would leave his home and join Mi Na on his travels. They would visit the world's great cities and make a fortune. Mi Na shook his head in shame. 'I must leave now,' he thought.

And just like that he packed his bag and left the following morning. One recollection of his travails mopping the floor at his restaurant spurred him on. 'I am not yet ready to hop on top of a mop. Ah, blasted poetry – how you flatter to deceive! The solution does not lie with words at all! Nor with anything comprised of them – theory and reason be damned!' It became his sole mission to find a tuk-tuk driver who would take him westwards to the monastery deep in the rainforest. In any case, there was no use in waiting for one, so Mi Na set off on foot to the west. Soon he was surrounded only by mountains and valleys and no people at all. When he passed someone who sold water or rice the dollars he offered them were met with bemusement. Mi Na possessed one hundred and fifty thousand of the local currency but decided not to spend it on water or rice. 'If I see a driver I will need every last bit of it,' he thought. A tuk-tuk driver rode past Mi Na and called out to him. He insisted on three hundred thousand of the local currency but this was too much for Mi Na. It was not because he deemed the value of his labour to be less than three hundred thousand but because he only had one hundred and fifty thousand. This fact was lost on many a driver until one old man in a vehicle that had seen better days pulled up by Mi Na. There were no longer roads at this stage of the route.

'One hundred thousand for you,' said Mi Na.

'OK,' replied the driver. 'Where?'

After some confusion about the purpose of a journey to a monastery, Mi Na had had enough. 'There is no reason for my journey. I simply must go to the monastery, at once!'

The tuk-tuk hurtled between potholes as the old man pushed his vehicle to its limit. Surrounded by motorcycles and scooters, the limitations of this beaten up tuk-tuk were all too clear. They rolled down a dusty track shrouded in its entirety by tree cover. Little light penetrated the force field of the forest though this did not deter the elderly driver who seemed to revel in the challenge. Eventually they rolled up limply to the foot of the monastery. Mi Na was covered from head to toe in orange dust. 'At least we made it by sundown,' he said to himself. He gave the driver a hundred thousand and he made off with it into the night. 'It is not Xeng Xong's fault,' thought Mi Na. 'After all, why must I burden those so young and innocent with the task of fulfilling my nightmarishly whimsical fetishes of the mind! Why ever would I do such a thing! Why, indeed.' His stream of consciousness was halted by chanting. A smooth melody slipped out of the temple and imbued Mi Na with a sense of peace unlike any he had experienced before.

A monk in an orange robe descended the steps of the temple and stood in front of Mi Na. 'You come to stay with us?' he asked.

'Yes, I came to stay with you.'

The monk studied the outsider through the darkness. 'You come to meditate with us?' he asked.

'Yes, I came to meditate with you.'

It was agreed that the best thing for Mi Na to do was wash himself and rest before the gong would sound several hours before sunrise the next day.

'What happens when I hear the gong?' asked Mi Na.

'You come to temple for morning prayer and meditation.'

By the time the gong sounded Mi Na had been lying awake for a while. He had spent the night cleaning himself as swiftly and thoroughly as the facilities permitted. A small bowl floated atop a larger bowl itself filled to the brim with water. This water would be replaced manually by the unsteady trickle of a rusty tap. The hole in the bathroom floor would function as a toilet. 'It is helpful that it flushes with two small bowlfuls of water,' thought Mi Na. He napped intermittently but had woken up each time with aches and pains. 'It is because I am not accustomed to sleeping on the floor,' he mused. 'I move in my sleep when I sleep in a bed because I will spring back into place from whichever position I please. Only when I can sleep on my back with total stillness will I awake pain-free.' All of these thoughts mingled in the mind of Mi Na against a cacophony of jungle noise louder than the noise of the island and louder still than the noise of the valley. He made his way from the hut to the temple by memory as only darkness pervaded the forest.

Upon reaching the temple Mi Na stopped in his tracks at the sound of a single monk chanting. 'I should enter slowly,' he thought. Climbing the stairs one by one a vast hall revealed itself to him, its walls adorned with all manner of decoration and splendour.

A large monk, who seemed to be an important figure in the monastery, sat at the front of the hall cross-legged, orange clad, his back to an array of dazzling paintings and statuettes. He looked across the hall at Mi Na. 'Welcome,' he said. There was nobody else in the temple. Mi Na bowed his head slightly and walked slowly towards the monk who had since averted his gaze and closed his eyes. 'Stop,' he said. Mi Na stopped. 'Sit,' he said. Mi Na sat. He mimicked the posture of the monk and closed his eyes. The hall filled with monks the gamut of shapes and sizes and they chanted together and they meditated together.

At the end of the service Mi Na approached the large monk who had been sitting at the front of the hall facing rows and rows of monks and a single line of nuns dressed in white. 'Thank you,' said Mi Na.

'At sun rise,' the large monk began, 'we collect alms from the village.' Mi Na could not conceal his excitement but this had been anticipated by his advisor. 'Not you. Not yet.' Mi

Na bore the look of a lost soul. 'You will go to the dining area. It is close to your hut. Instead of turning left as you leave, turn right. At the end of the path you will come to a clearing. The nuns will be preparing the kitchen and the tables for breakfast. They will show you what you need to do. When you have completed your chores you will join us for breakfast. It is important that you know you can spend your time here at the monastery as you please. After the gong sounds in the morning, there is only morning prayer and meditation, the alms walk, breakfast, lunch and afternoon prayer and meditation.' Mi Na nodded his head and thanked the large monk. 'Oh, and one more thing,' he went on. 'You must report at once to your neighbour's hut. He will shave your head. It is too hot to carry around all of that hair and besides you cannot keep it clean here.' Mi Na nodded his head and returned to his quarters to wash his face and have his head shaved.

Feeling decidedly fresher post-shave, Mi Na strode down the rainforest path and out into the dining area. Four stone tables stood in a row under a bamboo shelter. A wooden table was set up to one side, unsheltered by bamboo. The nuns waved Mi Na over to them with smiles as wide as the sun. 'Good morning,' said Mi Na.

The nuns laughed as one. 'No good morning for you!' Afraid of confusion striking as it had become accustomed to at the most inopportune moments of his journey, Mi Na simply stood and smiled. But for once no one was confused. 'You see the leaves?' asked the most elderly of the nuns. He could see the leaves. They were everywhere, covering the paths of the dining area, the tables and the stools. 'Sweep the leaves into the flowerbeds. Well, what are you waiting for! Here is the broom! Sweep!'

Mi Na took the broom in his hands and swept without blinking. His arms and legs pushed and pulled against the motion of the brush's bristles as though they were automated. In no time, the dining area was free of leaves.

The nuns were impressed and the most elderly of them presented Mi Na with a small banana. 'For night time. You are not allowed to eat then but you are new here. You will need it tonight.' Mi Na offered his hands to her and she put the banana in them. 'Now take it back to your hut! Quickly! Before the monks return from alms walk!' Mi Na did as he was told and returned to the dining area for breakfast. He sat in front of a large bowl of noodle soup with no chicken or pork or beef and savoured the scent of the coriander and chilli. A smaller bowl containing sticky rice was laid down next to him by the large monk. 'You did well today. Tomorrow you will walk with us. But first you must obtain the correct garments from your neighbour's hut. Please make sure you do this by nightfall.' Mi Na nodded. He chewed his noodles and slurped his soup and made sure he completed his sole remaining task of the day.

Many months went by and Mi Na arose to the sound of the gong several hours before sunrise. He attended morning prayer and meditation, collected alms from the village, ate breakfast and lunch with the other monks and attended afternoon prayer and meditation. After some time he stopped attending lunch for his stomach was still full with breakfast. He came and went as he pleased until one day the large monk took him to one side after morning prayer and meditation. 'How is meditation going for you, Mi Na?' It was going well aside from the pain so Mi Na told the large monk of the pain. 'Ah, yes, the pain. Now, when you experience the pain you will instinctively try to resist it. This is normal. But this does not have to be normal!' he laughed. 'So next time you feel the pain, dwell on the pain and the pain will cease.' Mi Na did as he was told and the large monk was right, the pain ceased, and it ceased sooner and sooner each and every time. Many more months went by and Mi Na decided it was time to go home. This time, however, he did not feel the urge to leave, nor did he wait to be washed by a wave of euphoria. Mi Na thought of nothing and every last sinew of his body was still. He returned home and swept the floor of his restaurant with his soul for all of eternity.

VIII

Strangers

———

They walked without a word
together through the night,
though neither felt the cold
as usually they might.

A figure in the fog
drifted across their path.
a-moment-and-a-half
Alas! The figure, gone.

For a feature or a manner
this figure was unclear.
A stranger, so she thought,
but not someone to fear.

We all begin as strangers,
she turned and said to him.
Friends and lovers we become,
the right match a small sum.

So be careful when you choose
with whom you'd like to dance.
That smile you went weak for
will be yours and just by chance.

He stared at her and nodded,
his mouth, he could not move.
Uncertain yet carefree,
she had nothing to prove.

He had wondered who she was
and why she had appeared.
Now he felt no urge to ask
such questions, no longer dear.

They walked without a word
together through the night,
though neither felt the cold
as usually they might.